The Secrets of the Powerful Crystal Gem

Tanish Prabhu

Melbourne Australia

Tanish Prabhu c/- Intertype Publish and Print
Unit 45, 125 Highbury Road
BURWOOD VIC 3125
Australia
www.intertype.com.au

Ordering Information:
Quantity sales. Special discounts are available on quantity purchases by corporations, associations, and others. For details, contact the "Special Sales Department" at the address above.

The Secrets of the Powerful Crystal Gem / Tanish Prabhu. —1st ed.
ISBN:978-0-6486131-9-0

CHAPTER 1

Light shines through his eyes as he slowly starts to wake up surrounded by nothing but empty white walls around him. He looks around to find an escape route and runs to a hollow pitch black room. However, he ends up in the same place he started causing him to fluster and panic from the situation. He screams for his parents and anyone that could help his way out but no answer comes his way. Then straight ahead of him appears a tall man in ancient robes and a long beard. In a short time, the kid walks towards him, itching for help. As he moves closer, he gets a good look at the man in front of him. The man welcomes him into his world and is told to follow him to a newer path. He asks the boy for personal information hoping that he remembers who he is. The boy's name is Daniel Steele, a 17 year old kid in high school confusingly wandering around without any knowledge of where he is. He has black hair and blue eyes and is a tall, built up figure. The two of them walked together. Daniel looked around, wondering where he was. All he could see was just a white background everywhere. The man introduced himself as Fro Jha, an old wise man, 400 years old and a peacekeeper from death and destruction. Fro Jha explained to Daniel the location he has been sent to. The place he called is Gemme, an ancient object created thousands of years ago and consists of infinite powers when used in the outside world but in the inside, it's a world known to be an afterlife, a place where all fallen soldiers live on and those who are destined to help come for their calling. Time moves relatively slower to that of time on earth. He mentioned to Daniel the events that occurred before he arrived. About two months ago, Daniel was led to an expected but unfortunate accident. His class went on an excursion to the caves in the regions of Victoria and inside the cave was a new room that was restricted from being accessed by anyone. In the restricted room, there was a shining bright blue light glowing under the door. When Daniel walked with the others, he saw the light under the door and was curious to go through and see it. He left himself behind the others and went into the restricted area. The light was so bright, it blocked his eyes from seeing anything, but as he got closer, Daniel went ahead and laid his fingers on the gem. The moment he touched it the ground shook and the walls and ceiling started to collapse. The gem's brightness decreased after it was touched and it just sat there, without moving. At this moment Daniel had no idea what to do.

Most of the students were searched for hours on end and some were declared dead while others were found responsive but injured. A search party went on the lookout for Daniel and by nightfall under the rocks and rubbles, Daniel was found, unresponsive but was still alive. His clothes and face were covered in dirt but he was comatose. A few hours later a helicopter arrived and Daniel was gently carried inside and flown back home to a hospital his family requested so they could be near him.

Daniel was flown to hospital and had not woken up since then. Daniel was starstruck, he thought of his friends and family and others who were part of the accident. He was told that his body is physically motionless but alive psychologically inside the gem. Daniel being led to believe his potential death was a dream. He tried to find another escape route but ended up finding Fro Jha yet again. He searched for answers as to how he would leave the place and get back into the real world where he would wake up and return to his normal life. Unfortunately, for him he was stuck. Jha told him his main purpose is to survive and train for threats and destruction because the gem he touched was his calling. In order for him to get back in the world, he had to train and fight any possible evil that came his way, hence he would not go back to live a normal life but a life in the complete opposite. Daniel was furious but he accepted his destiny. Daniel saw bright light covering his face and upon arrival, he saw what he perceived to be the afterlife. Birds flying in the same direction, big wave tides in the corner and internal peace everywhere. Jha led Daniel to a large white building up ahead on the hills. At the entrance, guards stood on both sides of the wall and made way for the two inside. The place inside was huge and spacious. There were pictures of people framed and placed on top of walls and statues of heroes built outside near the ocean. Jha stood in the middle of the place announcing that it's a place for peacekeepers like him. A job in the afterlife to keep peace in the new world. Jha pointed at the statues explaining that each generation had one being wielding the powers and it was overthrown by the next being the gem called for in the result of death from a specific weapon or otherwise. The gem had been studied in schools and universities for people who were interested in ancient history and archaeology.. He brought up a hologram of the object and showed him the gem itself, the most powerful object ever created in the universe.

This gem consisted of infinite powers and he informed Daniel that he has these powers and he is inside the gem. The thought of him having powers made him ask a lot of questions. He didn't believe himself to be someone he was expected to be. He looked at it all on the positive side knowing that he couldn't leave the world without being fully trained and given the knowledge of how to control his powers. They left the place and headed outside. There both Daniel and Fro Jha encountered a platform hidden on the ground that took them down. Underneath deep inside the gem was another room. The room had several weapons such as bombs and guns, training equipment, dummies and many more. Having looked at what he had to train with, Daniel approached a dummy. With his powers, the dummy left the ground and went into mid-air without Daniel realising he is in control. He grabbed out his hand and managed to get the dummy off the ground. He then clenched his fist to try and tear it apart but failed. The training facility is where Daniel had to learn to control his powers. Daniel became impatient and stubborn as he tried to tear the dummy apart. When he unclenched his fists and his palm was exposed, fire bolts started popping up Daniels's palm and was accidently thrown on the dummy. Daniel was alarmed and fell on a bunch of boxes behind him, looking at the fire in front of him. In his calm, soothing tone, Jha trained him for his first lesson of patience. Daniel is the type of kid who is determined to do anything. However, patience is not his strong suit. For the next several months, Daniel learnt his abilities and control. Every time he failed, he had to redo it again. He took several breaks to calm his mind until he was able to complete the task. Back in the training facility, he discovered spikes coming out of his fists. His aim was not great but he trained every day. Eventually, he was able to tear the dummy with his hands but still had a problem with his aim.

CHAPTER 2

3 months after the events in the cave, many victims suffered from breathing on rubble and debris. The city had high level asthma attacks not only from the explosion in the cave but the pollution from transportation. The hospital was crowded with sick and injured patients. Doctors and nurses running along to separate the sick and injured ones in separate rooms and levels. On level 3 arrived another patient. He was aided off the wheelchair and placed on the bed gently. The doctors were aiding another patient, whose name was Param Idle, another high school kid who injured himself in sport. He was in the same room as Daniel and learnt about his accident from the doctors. The nurse left the room to grab information of his details before his surgery. Param turned the TV on to avoid boredom but with nothing interesting on most channels, he turned to Daniel's unconscious body and decided to talk to him. Inside the gem, Daniel was meditating on shore, legs crossed and back straight. Wave tides coming in hard and birds chirping in the sky, but no sound could penetrate his mind. He trains to read the thoughts of others through his mind. He took continuous deep breaths and moments later he heard a voice. A voice slightly familiar but a new one. He concentrated on the person's mind and landed inside some of his memories to which he remembered who this kid was. "Param" Daniel mumbled. Daniel was then able to access the outside world and he saw his own body lying cold on the hospital bed. Daniel psychologically focused his mind out the window and saw the world he hoped to return to. It was broad daylight and inside the hospital, he focused his mind on Param who continued to talk about how he got his injury.

Daniel continued to listen to the voice. His consciousness seemed to intersect with Param's reality. As Param grappled with the inexplicable intrusion of Daniel's voice in his mind, a palpable tension filled the room, drawing the attention of by-standers and medical staff alike. Param's struggle to move his leg mirrored the internal conflict raging within him, his fear palpable as he confronted this unexplained phenomenon. Meanwhile, Daniel's attempt to maintain the connection fal-tered, leaving both him and Param grappling with the sudden disconnect. As soon as the connection broke off at the same time his mind led him to something else. He could see darkness somewhere else. A close-up figure but ambiguous in his mind. The figure growled. Its eyes are angry and yellow and a scar across its left eye. Daniel saw fear in himself and opened his eyes. He was told not to enter his mind elsewhere other than reality and he left the beach in a hurry. The doctors tried to calm Param down by injecting midazolam a sleeping injection that would allow him to relax but he pushed it away from him and told them he could hear a voice in his head although un-sure who it was, he kept repeating to them that a voice inside his mind knows his name.

Param was held back to relax and was injected on the arm. He eventually relaxed and went to sleep putting less stress on the doctors. Two of the doctors left the room while the third one kept watch. Inside the gem, Daniel ran back to the training facility where Jha was making a cup of herbal tea. Daniel fought hard to catch his breath. When Jha saw him he looked scared and Daniel explained what he saw. He mentioned he saw a kid with an injured leg named Param lying in the hospital. Someone he knows through school very briefly. He also was bothered by what he saw after that. Sudden darkness and inferiority. Un-ambiguous picture but he saw eyes that are not to be messed with and a growling sound. Jha was impressed with his ability to control but warned him to not fall for the dark side of it. Daniel demanded answers in what he feared to be a downfall but Jha wasn't worried. He went home leaving Daniel to fend in his own thoughts as he swam in the water to keep himself calm. Daniel was found by Jha sleeping on the beach in mid-air. It was early 7:30am and the sun was just rising. When he woke up, he was given a large stick called the baston, a battle weapon and was encountered by a guard who turned into an assassin on the beach.

He taught him ways of fighting threats not using powers. He lent him a weapon, a baston of a powerful stick that Daniel learnt to use. He was asked to go in a hand to hand duel with a guard assassin to increase his training and was told to concentrate on its weakness without power. The guard assassin came right at him and pounded Daniel to the ground. However, he managed to defend himself before getting a chance to attack. Although the assassin was strong, Daniel pushed him hard away from him and saw his weakness. He twirled his stick as soon as it came at him, then slightly punctured his lower body. The guard struggled to fight back and several minutes later, collapsed on the beach with Daniel having the higher ground. This impressed Jha and he saw the potential in Daniel. He and Jha continued walking back to the palace for a big meal before the rest of the training. Inside he read Daniel's face knowing he was interested and curious in the answers he wanted to find. Jha gave him a lecture to stay on the positive side of the line and to avoid the darkness. He later told him the cheat codes to get out of a fight quicker and weapons or powers to use in case of emergency.

CHAPTER 3

There was an announcement on the news right after the sport headlines that a certain object had been located at the site of the incident in the cave. The reporter announced that the object that investigators had found is a blue crystal gem. Diggers picked it up safely for testing and investigators also found blood in the same area they discovered the gem near the rubble. The TV was turned off soon after and there was a private discussion going on in the room in the underworld. An underworld run by gangs and criminals, some who are part of the black market. A man named Miles Henderson, 6,1 with a bulked up body. He has a long history of crimes committed over the last 10 years, some bigger than others. He brought together a group of experienced and the strongest members of his notorious, fearsome criminal gang. Over the 3 years, they have worked together to take down government systems, hunt down for the most precious gold in the mines of South East Asia and have nearly caused terrorist attacks before arriving in Melbourne where the gem is located. They are globally known as the Formidable Four. Miles was determined to hunt down the gem and access its powers which allowed him to seize control of the world, access government facilities by overthrowing the government and democracy. One of the members, Jasper Cryer doubted this mission, believing it to be a failed job in the near future. Jasper Cryer is one of their strongest members. A very muscular individual and is known to be an obnoxious person. He was notorious for the countless deaths of his own people after evidence in court found him secretly working with a new generation of the Sicilian mafia and had led to 350 people drugged and poisoned by him. He has been in and out of prison in the last 2 years for several other crimes he has been involved in but the mafia were never found on the grid.

Henderson made a bold plan to attack the building where the gem is being taken. He looked out the window and saw a shop that sold weapons and armoury. He explained how his plan would work out and trusted Lina woods and Jasper Cryer to assist him. Lina is a fearsome member. The only female and the youngest member but a hardcore fighter. with a dark backstory. She lived alone and fought for herself and her friends from the age of 12. Her parents were killed by a psychotic gunman who was later found dead from unknown circumstances. She trained in the martial arts 2 years later and completed her training and travelled around Europe where she completed the next part of her training. However, she was seen as the villain in her story when she was found guilty of the murder of her parents. Although she claimed to be innocent, all evidence went against her. Tension hung heavy in the air like a thick fog. Henderson although wanted more control of this object, he had someone who was more interested. His declaration of personal gain echoed against the walls, a stark contrast to the purported mission's objectives and chose to forget his boss's words. Meanwhile, Mason, with his quiet demeanour and blood-stained knuckles, observed the unfolding drama with a silent intensity, his mind undoubtedly calculating every move. Jasper's inquiry about Hunter's abrupt disappearance only added to the mounting intrigue, hinting at underlying motives and allegiances yet to be revealed. Hunter is the most mysterious but the smartest individual in the group. He tends to get by, by solving the most simple and complex tasks, and he has never been caught or found for his crimes. Unknown about his whereabouts, disappearance for days, betrayer to others, the list goes on and he usually prefers to work alone. He walked closer to Jasper who slowly went to grab his knife. The tension in the room was palpable as Miles Henderson's ominous words to take control of the world as his own hung in the air, casting a shadow over the group. Miles's plan had been called into question, leaving doubt and uncertainty in its wake for someone who committed the most impossible crimes, this one is the most impossible. His credibility had been called into question, leaving the group divided and uncertain of their next move. But amidst the chaos and uncertainty, one thing remained clear, the need for vigilance and unity in the face of looming threats. As the day wore on and shadows lengthened, Jasper and Lina found themselves drawn deeper into a web of intrigue and danger, their paths converging with those of shadowy figures and hidden agendas. But with their bond forged in trust and determination, they faced the challenges ahead with unwavering resolve, knowing that together, they were stronger than any obstacle they might encounter. They found themselves immersed in their own world as they wandered through the bustling market, their playful banter and shared laughter a stark contrast to the grim realities unfolding around them. But even in their moments of levity, Jasper remained vigilant, his senses attuned to any signs of trouble or deception. As they strolled through the market, Jasper's keen eyes caught sight of Hunter Mason engaging in suspicious dealings with three individuals, his instincts immediately on high alert. Sensing the need to investigate further, Jasper gently extricated himself from Lina's side, his focus shifting to the unfolding scene before him. With a silent nod to Lina, Jasper moved with purpose, his steps deliberate as he discreetly followed Hunter and his associates, his senses sharp and his mind racing with possibilities. He knew that danger lurked around every corner, and he was determined to uncover the truth before it was too late.

As Daniel stood within the breathtaking beauty of the gem, its serene atmosphere in front of him like a warm embrace, he couldn't help but feel a pang of reluctance at the thought of leaving. The world within the gem seemed to radiate with peace and harmony, a stark contrast to the chaos and uncertainty of the real world. But duty called, and Daniel knew that he couldn't remain within the confines of the gem forever. With a heavy heart, he focused his thoughts on the task ahead, his mind filled with memories of his training and the lessons he had learned during his time within the gem. As the sun dipped below the horizon and the wind picked up around him, Daniel felt the warmth of the sand beneath his feet, a comforting reminder of the power he held within him. With each passing moment, he felt a sense of calm wash over him, his mind clear and focused as he prepared to return to reality. Suddenly, a familiar voice echoed in his mind, the soft, sweet tones of his older sister Molly. His heart skipped a beat as he watched her departure from their home, accompanied by her cousin Will. Concern etched itself onto Daniel's features as he observed the scene unfold before him, his thoughts racing with worry for his sister's well-being.

Daniel's mind shifted to the hospital. The same one his physical body lying in the hospital and he sees his dad Michael standing beside him. He had talked to him, hoping he'd wake up sooner. His father had touched his hand. It was cold, almost frozen. He left the room and joined Molly and William into another room 9B next door. Soon he lost concentration and wasn't able to continue his joy of watching his family who were nearby. He realised his mother's having a baby but reading her mind she felt sad and alone. Back in the gem, tears run down Daniel's eyes. The wall of water becomes an ocean once again and Daniel opens his eyes and goes down on his knees crying. Jha appears behind him placing his shoulder on Daniel's hand. Daniel's voice breaks and gets emotional mentioning how much he misses his family and the loneliness he feels although he had to commit to his destiny. Jha encouraged him to get back up to his feet and continue his training but gave him a short break. Daniel looks at the ocean view gazing at the sun and the waves tides. He convinces Jha he is ready to go back, he is ready to protect and fight for what is coming. Jha smiles. He nods and agrees that he has been able to control his powers for the last 8 months. Straight ahead appeared in the distance is a simple white door. Jha was convinced that Daniel was ready the moment he showed patience and was able to control. Daniel walks up to Jha and shakes his hand and is told to reach out for any trouble. Daniel walks through the door, his psychological form never to be seen again.

CHAPTER 4

Daniel wakes up on the hospital bed, the same place his body has been lying on for 8 and a half months. The sun shining right into his eyes through the window on his left. He gets up and sits on the edge of the bed. He feels a bump on his chest as he gets up. He finds a mirror that's placed next to him and pulls his hospital robes up leaving him horrified at first. In the middle of his chest is a large blue crystal gem attached to him that connects him with his powers and the beyond. As he walks over he feels uncomfortable with the weight of the gem. He gets used it as he walks in his room from one end to another, does some push ups and sit ups and bends up and down to adjust himself from any early pain. One of the doctors walked by and noticed him staring at the window, standing still. Daniel leaves the room and heads next door to 9C, the room number he saw in his mind. It was empty. No one was there. The clock struck 10am. The same doctor from the previous room followed behind him. she gently approaches him and briefly explains to him about the birth of his new baby brother, Juan Steele. When he found out his new brother was born 2 days ago, he was devastated to not be there but he was also happy. It solves one problem of his where the entire family met up in the next room before Daniel lost concentration. His mother named his brother Juan Steele and he was born at 11pm. The doctor described the baby as handsome after delivery and she offered to accommodate him before he was cleared to leave. Her tag name was Charli Smith. She is tall, young and an attractive woman, probably in her early 30s. She sat him down and placed a breakfast burger in front of him and gave him the bag that she kept all those months. Inside Daniel found his original belongings he had with him before the accident which included his phone and his wallet. She explained to him that he had been in critical condition and unmovable for nearly 8 months which later reminded Daniel the state of time in the gem compared to back on earth.

She asked Daniel the events he remembered before he went into a coma. Daniel was quiet at first. He tried to get the correct words out of him. He couldn't tell her the truth of his powers or the gem he was inside because no one would believe him, cleverly stating that he felt like he was in another world, trapped and lonely. Charli continued to ask Daniel questions but his mind shifted elsewhere. He went inside her mind for observation and lost focus on reality. He was warned to not use his powers in front of anyone in the outside world and keep his identity a secret. Charli was curious to know the dream he was in but Daniel was in the middle of her surfing her mind and saw light in her more than the darkness. He pulled his mind out of hers and stopped the questioning. Breaking the rules immediately, he cloned himself. 5 clones surrounded Charli and himself. Charli's body froze still, unable to move or twitch. The clones were a distraction to escape and they disappeared allowing Daniel to place two fingers on her head to wipe that exact memory from her mind, leaving the hospital without anyone else knowing. Daniel walked out the door with the sun beaming right at his face. He found a small alleyway near Church street and decided to walk around there to go home. He found a wall in front of him and went through it, instantly approaching a bar. He spent a few minutes inside, watching sports and eating some food before his senses noticed something unusual. 3 men walked in, dressed in casual shirts and pants.

All 3 loaded with guns scanned by Daniel with extra vision. One of them pulled their guns out and threatened to shoot everyone if they didn't get their money. Daniel shape shifted into a different person, someone older to avoid being caught as a kid. He got out of his seat and left the place but was hauled by the 3 guys. All 3 came at him but didn't stand a chance in the fight, knocked out immediately onto the ground and he left the place. Daniel spent the night in his aunt's garage in the city on Toorak road without anyone in the house noticing. He chose to not see his family because of the situation he was in and his purpose. The traffic was not smooth at 11pm at night and it was extremely loud. Daniel was half asleep when he heard his Aunt's voice helping a crying baby which was Juan. Daniel reflected on his chances of meeting his little brother while lying on a comfortable couch. He sensed they were coming in and quickly ran up to the roof, sitting there and staring at the sky. He looked down the window later on and saw the family who believed him to be potentially dead. He smiled and moved in the corner, gliding in the air and sleeping in the cold. Daniel walked away the next day exploring. He arrived at his school which he missed out on for 8 straight months and decided to walk to meet his friends and teachers. He saw one guy talking to another person outside the front gate and was spotted by him soon after. He had a priceless reaction when he saw Daniel outside the gate and ran to hug him for a few straight minutes. Clayton, his best friend and most trusted individual reunited with Daniel and the two spent time talking.

Clayton was at the gate with his food he ordered online and walked back to school , taking Daniel with him to see the others. At the oval, they spotted another mate, Marcus Watson, brown hair, short and leaning on a wall looking at his phone. He dropped his phone when he saw Daniel and nearly fainted. As Daniel walked around, people started to appear. People who knew Daniel closely. A whole group of year 11s gathered around him. They joyfully clapped and cheered for his return. Teachers came out as well, curious to see a whole crowd gather around like someone got into a fight. Daniel was hugged, grabbed and carried, surrounded by people who wanted to know what happened. He never told them the truth, stating he had no idea what got him into the hospital in the first place. Daniel felt everyone's mind. He could control it but he felt an awkward presence near him, an ambiguous dark soul creeping near and near but shook his head and forgot about it. He spotted a teacher ahead who was staring at him. Daniel went to him. They shook hands. A shed of tears came down his eyes and he smiled. His name was Rene Turgis, the teacher that led the excursion to the caves in Nelson, Victoria, where it all began for Daniel. Mr Turgis and Daniel walked together inside and headed to his office.

He locked the door and shut the drapes. When asked how he felt when he woke up from hospital, Daniel gave a subtle reply, without being hesitant he described his return from a coma induced state as positively thrilling, a second chance at life to make up from the number of months he missed. After their long chat Daniel headed off outside before his first class in months. He spotted a beautiful girl sitting on the side in the hallway, scrolling through her phone with her friends. Daniel smiled and walked to her. She looked up and they reunited after 8 months. Her name was Anya Hart, a tall girl with long dazzling jet black hair. They reunited after months and spent a few hours together. They had a long conversation for a while about everything that happened. Anya was there that day. She survived the event and only had a broken arm. Along with her injury, the loss of Daniel, which sent her into depression at which point she didn't go back to school for 2 months and started to have bulimia. She resolved her pain by seeing a therapist that made her better and after a few months, she moved on from her problems with the medication she was given and outdoor activities she was involved in.

CHAPTER 5

D aniel woke up with the same nightmare for the past week, reliving unclear visions of those eyes he saw while inside the gem. He stayed at his friend Clayton's house for a few weeks after telling him that he was not ready to visit his family. Every morning before breakfast Daniel drew the same picture of the yellow eyes and the scar that comes with it while Clayton kept talking about his girlfriend Maya he's gone out with for 2 months. The two laughed about their problems while doing their own personal things. Daniel also drew another figure he uncovered that is slightly unclear to him. He sat on his chair for his midday class, resting his head on the window looking at the cars going by on Domain street and the year 9s running laps in their PE class. It wasn't hard to get distracted by the loud noise from the PE teacher who already started yelling at 3 boys for breaking the rules with the equipment. Suddenly, his mind shifted to several noises. He heard a crash and his mind had the full image of the incident. It was inside a museum. During the break, Daniel scrolled on his phone and read over the headline 'hostage situation" The thought came to Daniel's mind that this was his chance to help the people. Straight after class he skipped math, ran off, out the gates and over at Clayton's house. He was not able to get in the front door jumped through the upper window and into Clayton's room. He turned the TV on to see the bigger picture and saw the news of an alert at the museum that four armed people have taken control of the museum and were looking for an object.

Daniel was not too worried but the thought of him having powers allowed him to interfere with situations like this. He put on a hoodie over his clothes and covered his face to avoid being exposed and designed a helmet that he is able to create by the gem to cover his face. The helmet allows him to see where he is going. The gem shields the helmet from being damaged from anything and the crystal created by the gem inside controls and modifies the helmet automatically. Daniel flew out of the window and made himself less visible, allowing him to track the place and the culprits faster. In the museum, Miles took control of the hostages, 10 of them who were on the verge of death. Cryer and Lina took care of the swarm of police outside the National Gallery Museum and 5 policemen were wounded from the attacks. It was difficult to attack both of them with high level combat training and therefore the scene became bloody. Miles showed no mercy, quickly shooting two people inside as he took control. He demanded answers asking for an ancient object known to be the gem. The hostages on the floor were convinced he was a mad man. claiming the gem to be a myth from ancient times. The gem he wanted ended up being a replica he stole.

This made Miles even more furious and immediately shot him without any care. The body of the man lay cold on the floor hinting a moment of silence. They all heard a noise in the background. shattered glass nearby. Jasper Cryer went off to search who entered the museum. He drew his gun and walked slowly to the dinosaur exhibit. On his right he saw a moving shadow run past and immediately started shooting. The same went on his right. Daniel's shadow slowly crept out, however could not be seen visibly. He produced a large amount of smoke out of his hands that prevented Jasper from shooting. He aimed in the wrong direction allowing Daniel to pull up from behind and trapped Jasper on a wall with two webbed spikes landing on his shoulders and he was unable to move. Daniel's shadow continued to be visible in the smoke. It made Jasper question what he saw and he desperately tried to escape from the wall screaming in pain as the webs had acid spreading on both his shoulders. Daniel questioned him about the hostage situation. The encryption from the crystal made his voice grow deeper. Jasper told him everything and gave him the directions. Daniel found the hostages, two already dead and the rest alive but shaken. He was spotted by Miles who immediately pointed his gun at him. Daniel defended himself from the bullets coming straight at him. He even stopped the bullets mid-air, crushed them and they fell on the ground increasing Miles' misery and convinced himself of the bluff the man he shot told him. Metal spikes burst out of Daniel's knuckles right in the centre of the hole that blew the gun up.

Miles was pounded to the ground and his two companions went up against him. Hunter Mason stabbed him with his brass knuckles and there was a deep cut on his ribs. Daniel was able to heal the injury quickly due to the power of immortality and quick healing. This shocked Hunter as he threw away his weapon and punched him right in the abdomen. Daniel flew right into a stack of boxes but jumped out momentarily and grabbed him in the air from a far distance. Hunter's face became purple and he fell on the ground coughing. He looked up at Daniel terrified at what he was up against. His heart beat rapidly and got thrown straight into a wall but did not stand down. Daniel clapped both his hands together and the wind pushed Hunter out of the museum through the window and fell into the river. Daniel ran off to find the gem but saw a sharp piece of wood on his shoulder. He took it out feeling the pain while his shoulder healed back quickly. On his way to securing the replica gem he was hauled by Lina Woods. Half her face was covered with bandana with only the eyes seen. The two fought in a very long battle.

Daniel's baston had a blade appearing on both sides and he went up against the two daggers Lina had. The two went into battle, going at it at arm's length. Daniel stabbed her in the knee with one blade and threw her with the stick. She landed on both her feet and came real fast at him but her fist landed on the shield covering Daniel which pushed her right back into a wall. She held on, jumping right at him but her hair was grabbed and she thrown right on the ground. Daniel stood up to scan the location of the replica gem. He appeared in front of Lina who was puffing in pain. Lina's full face was exposed after her bandana fell into her hands. Daniel recognised who she was, remembering her name instantly. He could not get the right words out of his mouth. He was lost, trembling in fear. He left Lina lying on the ground and was notified the gem had been located in the next room. He saw Miles break the window to grab the gem and was convinced it would light up. Daniel stalled him and Miles ran at him however failed to survive the attack. He shielded himself while Miles disappeared, grabbing the fake gem that was on the ground and freeing the hostages.

CHAPTER 6

Miles was frustrated. When he questioned Jasper Cryer, he struggled to find the right words and his frustrations grew on everyone else. Lina sat by the window stitching her knee. She looked at Miles whose face started to burst. She looked at him upset and angry, claiming no information on her situation. She was bothered by how Daniel knew her name and went into deep thought about what she could have done better to win her next battle. Miles took a few sips of his drink and looked at his partners. He came up with a new plan on the spot that involved hunting down Daniel or in their case the unknown shadow. He took the device that tracks certain objects which was created a few days ago that he stole from the lab in a subtle break in. He placed a tracker on the replica gem seconds before it was stolen and the blue dot beeped in the middle convincing himself that the gem was not a myth. The next day the local newspaper popped outside the door. Clayton's mum, Kirby Simmons brought it inside to have a read while having a cup of tea. She found a peculiar headline on page 2 and discussed it with her husband Eric before he went to work. The headline stated *"Vigilante on the loose"* The picture displayed a figure in a hood and a mask standing on the roof of the national museum looking down. Clayton saw the same news his mother had seen but on his phone and showed it to Daniel. Daniel was scared and sweated as he read the article. The unexposed version of him spotted by journalists during his escape from the building meant the other version of him exists. Two pages of incrimination and blame towards him for something he did the opposite. The signs that led people to believe the worst is yet to come. There were talks on the tram and on the streets on the way to school. It kept Daniel quiet as he secretly is a so-called criminal although the full story is not shown. Luckily, for him he wasn't exposed but the police are on the search for two different criminals.

They already are investigating Miles and others known to be the Formidable Four according to this morning's news on TV but also another criminal unknown and "out of the blue" according to the first sentence of the article. On his way to class, Daniel was hauled by his maths teacher, Mr Marshall who gave him detention at lunch for skipping class before the end of the day. Mr Marshall is a strict math teacher who has high expectations and sets standards for his students and does not let go of any mistake made. When he stopped Daniel his face turned redder than a tomato and was pissed at him, angrily noting that he will send an email to Daniel's guardians and notify them of the issue. The evening that very same day after a hectic afternoon of screaming and tension in the classroom during detention, Daniel, Clayton and Anya attended Friday night football at the MCG. The atmosphere was electric and the majority of the crowd wore jackets and jumpers as it was a cold night. The crowd outside the MCG was packed. They sat on the second floor with perfect seats watching the game from a clear view. The crowd was energetic as Collingwood took the lead in the first half. The police appeared to kick out a few fans who became drunk and started fighting as the second quarter came to an end. During the half time break, Daniel was slowly spotted by a number of familiar people he saw at the bar a few weeks back and they were observing him.

One of them had a tracker and the dot beeping right towards the gem inside his bag. Daniel looked on both sides as he saw more men than before creeping towards him and he had no time to form a plan, preventing him from figuring out who they were and left the stadium at half time. When he reached the exit he placed his hoodie over his head and the real gem activated the chip. The 3 men followed him outside the MCG but Daniel disappeared, popping up behind them and were taken down easily once again. Daniel then ran off to the bridge where he was surrounded by 4 of them who tracked him down. In the background the siren went off for the second half of the quarter. Daniel was surrounded, quickly thinking of his new plan. He then saw a moving train come in his direction straight ahead of him right opposite 2 of the men. He ran towards them, jumped, kicked the first guy long haired guy and punched the other with full arm tattoos. One fully armed man headed to his right, punched him in the stomach and threw him down the stairs. Daniel flew right into him and headed for the incoming train. The last man left standing had the tracker, pointed a gun right at him and shot him multiple times but Daniel escaped them and jumped straight on top of the train. The same man with the gun continued shooting him but Daniel was unable to be seen and therefore he jumped right on the train expecting to find Daniel inside. He destroyed the window and jumped in-side the train. On the inside it was empty. No one sat in there and he continued to search inside, gun pointed out. There was a moment's silence for a fair few minutes.

The shooter bumped into a teenager wearing ear pods on another platform. When the shooter turned his back, he was gone with only the ear pods sitting there. There was a moment of silence for a good few minutes until it was broken.

"I was hoping you wouldn't follow me." The voice came from behind.

The shooter saw his mask clear as day and released the trig-ger but the bullet was stopped and vibrated in the air through Daniel's mind. It broke into several pieces and he lifted the shooter up and threw him out the window into the Yarra river. Daniel reached Flinders Street Station two minutes later and hopped off the train. He took his hoodie off and the crystal turned off his chip. He hid by the wall and peaked out in the darkness to check if he was still being followed. No sight of movement and he found a nearby food shop and went off to buy himself dinner. Finally, Clayton and Anya appeared and found Daniel buying a sandwich. Both looked worried and saw his jumper with holes. Daniel told them he ran into a personal situation, hiding the real truth away from the two of them. Clayton went home while Daniel and Anya spent a couple of hours together sitting on the grass and watching the river. Anya looked worried and asked him several questions about his disappearance, listening to Daniel lie about everything she believed to be true about the phone call on a personal matter. He watched the lights ahead and the shooter's body lying in the water, moving slowly as the water moved which only Daniel could see from afar with the power to scan and see from far. Saturday afternoon, Daniel went for a walk in Port Melbourne. It was a warm afternoon and the forecast showed no rain so a lot of people appeared on the beach and the traffic was busy. Unsure of how he was found by a bunch of thieves and shooters the night before, he created a new plan which was to track Lina Woods in his mind which would lead to the men and the situation. Daniel took his clothes off and walked into the shallowness of the water.

His feet felt the sting of freezing water as he continued to walk into the deeper ends. One of the powers that Daniel possessed was immortality so if he ever decided to relax his mind underwater without any distractions from the surface, he would do so. Instead, Daniel made himself less visible on the surface and floated in the middle of the depth of the ocean as the water gave him peace. He created a shield around him to avoid the waves from touching him and throwing him into the water as a sign of distraction. Daniel closed his eyes and went into deep thought. Not long after he found Lina on a train to Heidelberg. He entered her thoughts to which he realised she was going to some training facility close to where she lived. Daniel opened his eyes and flew back on the beach. He took the next arrival tram to Flinders Street Station. After a hard thought of his current situation, Daniel went home to secure the replica gem in a box and hid it under his bed, grabbed his bag and went on the next platform that took him to Heidelberg. The Journey was an hour and 45 minutes from the city. The train was half full as the clock approached at 6pm. He looked out the window as the sun went down quickly as the train made its final stop.

Daniel left the station in a hurry as rain came down heavily completely wetting his clothes. His mind located Lina in a gym in a quiet area near the town and away from the city. He approached the gym which was closed and dark inside. The door was fully shut so Daniel phased through it. He found the light switch and the place became bright. His eyes tracked down a small passage under the carpet. This door led him down a passageway and he found an underground training facility. Daniel was alone but the noises became louder. The room was pitch black and he heard a voice echoing across the room. The darkness prevented his eyes from scanning the area around him even with the mask on. Daniel walked slowly in the room listening to anything that was moving around him. He heard the sound of a weapon and little chants. Behind him was a small amount of light and the flame dropped. It circled around Daniel and he was surrounded by a group of assassins. Opposite him was a certain individual whom Daniel wanted to meet. He tried to escape his way out to which he failed as the assassin's weapon aggressively pointed towards him. "One move and even your powers wouldn't last against them. The footsteps became louder as they approached him. The shadow was visible through the flame and it got bigger each moment. The danger and death bestowed upon his eyes and right before the attack appeared Lina Woods. Daniel fell into a crisis as he was not able to do anything. His helmet scanned the assassins around him realising the danger to his powers.

CHAPTER 7

Daniel left the gem before he was trained to see in the dark and through it. He believed his chances of survival were more difficult. However, he remembers Jha explaining to him that under any pressure he was able to control his mind and focus on the situation in front of him. He was challenged to a duel where if he lost, his powers would be taken away from him. He shape shifted into one of the assassins and moved backwards into the shadows where he became free. Under Lina's command the assassins left and the flame faded out. Lina took out her blade to aim right into Daniel but it went straight onto the wall. Daniel's ghosting disappearance haunted Lina and he remained in the shadows of the pitch black room and slowly walked around the room and right behind Lina. He used his mind to grab the brass knuckle hidden in her pocket and used the opportunity for distraction. Meanwhile Lina closed her eyes and heard the small footsteps from behind her. When the opportunity came she stabbed him straight in the ribs leading her to believe it was one of her assassins who was under Daniel's control. It was not an easy way out for Daniel considering he is facing a highly trained assassin, however, he took a risky approach. While Lina ran into the next room searching for a certain weapon that would win her the battle, Daniel was nowhere to be seen. Lina was alone in the room. The baston she pulled out had a blade on the tip that can kill certain beings and takes away its power. She could hear movement around the walls and the sound grew bigger. The shadow was spotted. It was powerful and what came out of it was a ball of fire. It missed her by inches. There was a moment of silence before she saw a fake assassin lurking behind her. He stood still waiting for the attack to come straight to him. Lina ran straight at him but damaged the wall in the room. Daniel appeared on the other side of the room and took out his powerful baston, the weapon that creates mass destruction and has various effects and features.

There was a moment of silence before it was broken by Daniel's voice. He got through to Lina's mind to distract her from her victory. "Death is your only solution, he whispered. The easiest way out is through your emotions, I know who you are." Daniel read her mind clearly. He saw the treatment she was given in her early stages when she first arrived for training, the mark she got when she was given the name 'Black whisper,' the deadly name and sound that puts fear in her enemies' mind and would distract them from fighting back unless they are brave. Before that her old life and the pain she went through as a child. Lina looked around for the voice that was speaking to her. She shook her head when she realised it was him. "Get out of my head you piece of shit." The duel went on before Daniel's electric current that came out of his baston rebounded off hers right into him. He got electrocuted by his own power and fell right onto his knees. Lina moved closer to him and took off his disguise only to see nothing. She was furious and took out her blade and threw it on the wall. "I am everywhere and nowhere, in the shadows or just watching you from afar. You will never touch me or hurt me, no matter how strong you are." The voice faded. Outside the rain poured heavily onto the ground. Daniel left the gym and was almost on the brink of collapse. The blue current spread around him like fire. He could not fight back from this situation and decided to fly his way back home. However, his legs struggled to stay in the air due to the electrocution that rebounded right back at him during the fight. He arrived in the city in the middle of the night but passed out immediately and landed straight into the Yarra river. The sound of the water was so loud it alarmed everyone on the bridge and people near the river in the middle of the night, however no one ever knew who or what fell in. Daniel reached the surface the next morning at around 8am. He got out of the river and laid straight on the grass gasping for breath. His clothes were wet and covered with dirt that was inside the water. He went to the nearest shop to find some fresh clothes to wear. It was a foggy, icy morning so he put on a jumper. On the bridge he saw a news reporter and a cameraman from a distance and listened to the witnesses being asked several questions about the incident, however his mind shifted to a more important thing ahead of him. He found a cafe on Swanston street and ordered a large cup of tea where he sat down and drank it while his body was still shivering from the cold, freezing unclean water he fell into when the energy from his weapon drained out his ability to fly home.

In the cafe he saw Clayton's girlfriend Maya talk with the guy who was working at the counter. She wore a blue dress and heels so it seemed she was at some party the night before. She laughed in a conversation they had and they kissed as she leaned in at the counter. The guilt went down Daniel's body when he realised he had to confess the truth to Clayton, his best friend and the person who he lives with until he decides to meet his real family again. When she turned around, the smile on her face changed and was scared when she saw Daniel. He waved at her with an awkward reaction and her face turned red. She walked clumsily out of the door, probably still tired or getting through a hangover which didn't surprise Daniel and he followed her till flinders. Maya is one of the smartest people known but irresponsible. Her addiction to drinking began months ago after her parents' divorce and she blamed everyone for her actions. Her relationship with Clayton is toxic, so toxic it gets to the point where drinking leads to continuous cheating on Clayton which has been happening for a while, although she denied it the first time she was asked nearly 2 weeks ago. Daniel questioned the situation and she started crying as she waited for a tram. He saw the guilt in her eyes but when he read her mind she was wrapped up about the kiss that happened moments ago. While Daniel was interested in talking, Maya forcefully refused. She stormed on the tram angry and frustrated. However, it wasn't Daniel's biggest concern. He spent his first two free periods roaming around the city.

He remembered some of the events from last night and felt a sting of power flow through his body. He knew he'd lost the duel but left the place without having to give up his powers or his life, but he does not understand how the current rebounded back at him and affected him. He felt his right hand shake unusually as the current started zapping out. He couldn't control it and moments later accidentally aimed at a building. The damage of the building caught the attention of many people. This made Daniel panic. The damage was limited but it caused 5 injuries on the ground. Daniel was unseen by anyone and successfully made himself clear from the situation in order to control the current coming out of his body, especially his hand. When he sat back at the cafe he panicked and closed his eyes, taking deep breaths. He needed to reach out to the gem to interact with Fro Jha on his current situation. He also had another problem he wanted to solve at home. He looked at the number of messages on his phone from Clayton and Marcus over the last 6 hours. He ignored the messages and put his phone away. Daniel looked around for any suspicious acts from people around him, especially people wearing suits and holding guns that nearly got him caught last time. He caught a tram to get home.

When he got home he found Clayton's mum, Kirby Simmons in the kitchen and his father Erik Mitchell reading a newspaper at the breakfast table. The news was on in the background. Clayton's mum questioned the whereabouts of Daniel this morning after his absence yesterday evening and throughout the night. Daniel came up with a quick lie on the spot, bringing up his sister who claimed he searched for an entire night and how he wanted to see her to which they believed. In reality, he asked them for a favour to reach out to his sister. It would be alarming if he messaged Molly out of the blue after and a half months in the hospital. Daniel talked with his guardians and was made breakfast before his first actual class in an hour. They were happy to see him take the stand and meet one of the members of his family and therefore, Kirby Simmons made the call. Daniel met up with Clayton and Anya who lined up in the cafe at school among others in a huge line. Both of them discussed the news from the event that occurred moments ago as well as the problem that occurred in the Yarra. A theory believed by Anya is that the unknown lurking around threw a dead body in the river. She mentioned a body from a few nights ago floating on the surface of the river. On the other side, someone screamed for help as the body went past them. Clayton believed that the mist sounds like a better name for this thug because of his sudden disappearance and the ability to not be seen easily in fights. Accurate name for someone who hides himself in a mask without being exposed and can't be seen half the time for more than 5 seconds." The thought of the name struck Daniel's mind and he liked it. In class, Daniel paid less attention to the subject and more about his hand still unusually shaking for a long period of time. He looked out of the window and saw several police cars drive past the school and an ambulance too, driving to the city to help out the injured people in the crash site. But just in the corner, he could see a tall woman hiding in the alleyway, grabbing out her blade in case anyone followed her. Her cover was not exposed with the mask she wore. It was Lina herself recognised through a scan from afar. Daniel couldn't reach her mind nor could leave the class in person after his first warning. He had the ability to clone himself but instead used the chip that controls his mask to spy on her whereabouts. He opened the window and let the chip do its thing while he turned on the computer to see the whole situation at hand.

Lina was seen killing each person and looking for answers she was desperate for but he could not hear. Luckily for him the chip that followed her has a recording button that allows him to hear what she is looking for. She went upstairs and was joined by Jasper Cryer. Looking from the computer, the other two, Hunter Mason and Mile's Henderson were nowhere to be seen. It was a club in the alleyway and they both sat down to discuss their business. Daniel failed to see the whole show as the bell rang for break time. He was however asked to stay behind to discuss with his teacher about his assessment that was explained. She looked a bit concerned but confident enough when Daniel explained his essay plans. He promised that he would complete his assignment by the due date. He left the classroom and joined the others on the school ground. The chip flew back inside and Daniel hid it in his pocket. At the assembly, everyone was asked to meet in the hall to discuss a very important message. Clayton and Daniel bumped right into Maya. She was eager to leave when she saw both of them but the line was incredibly long and slow to get in. Anya joined them but gave an angry look at Maya, knowing that she had information she wanted to share but was not allowed. The same went for Daniel while Clayton was incredibly happy to see her. When they all went in, Daniel and Anya talked about their relationship and each shared the information. Anya surprisingly didn't expect anything to come out of Daniel until he told her this morning's talk. She and Maya have been good friends for years. They both saw Clayton hugging her and looked happy and were concerned about him when both of them came into the same section Daniel and Anya sat in. Principal Bell arrived on the stage looking furious than ever. First she talked about the mess in the bathrooms that she wanted solved immediately but that wasn't her biggest problem. The topic about the unknown lurker came up and for 20 minutes she talked about the safety and wellbeing of the people. She mentioned the lurker roamed in her own street two nights ago in Heidelberg and caught a slight glimpse of him outside the gym. This made Daniel question his situation. He didn't wear his hood or mask when he came out of the gym. He'd be expelled from school and exposed for his actions that people would believe to be bad. She claimed the lurker to be dangerous and suspicious and explained the reasons behind it. He dropped one body in the river a couple of weeks ago and another body fell into the river last night but nobody ever saw it. This morning a suspicious blue lightning came out of nowhere and hit a building. Principal Bell called special forces to catch him and send him away. She pointed to the screen which showed her phone number. The principle was loud like she made her statement and her points. Her tone was sincere and determined and she wasn't hesitant to find out the identity of the lurker. Daniel went into thought of clearing the memory of her mind and everyone else's to avoid the whole situation. The audience around him and everywhere else whispered to each other about what principle Bell said, including Daniel's own friends. Daniel's face turned red and had to keep his cover from being blown but made a fatal mistake by opening his mouth. He got up and defended the lurker or himself, calling the lurker a good guy and a hero for his actions.

He caught everyone's attention including the principal. Daniel's response to the questioning about the mysterious figure known as the Lurker was poised and carefully crafted, reflecting his adeptness at navigating delicate situations. He avoided directly condemning the Lurker as a criminal, instead suggesting a deeper, more altruistic purpose behind their actions. His theory hinted at a belief in redemption and justice, painting the Lurker as a force for good in a city plagued by notorious criminals like the formidable four. The whole meeting was over and Principal Bell looked for Daniel in the line but disappeared. The trio finished school early. While Anya stayed back to study, Daniel and Clayton went home. It allowed Daniel to listen to the recording and to meet up with his sister which Daniel mentioned on the way. The two talked about sport for a while and on the way home Daniel's instincts kicked in straight away. There was a moment of silence when the two stopped walking. Daniel's surroundings were clear for a short time. Right in the moment was the sound of a blade flying straight at Daniel and Clayton and Daniel caught the blade through his instincts and sound. Right at that point, Mason knew who he was fighting against. The fear went through Clayton when he saw him catch the blade. His body froze all the way and started to panic. On the top of the house opposite them was a man who looked down at both of them. He jumped right down and came straight at the two, knocking out Clayton who fell right into a tree but couldn't spot Daniel himself. He went missing in clear daylight but came back more visible, not fully exposed to the enemy. He ran straight at him but instead punched the bark of a tree, making a hole right in the middle. There was a moment of silence before he turned around and right behind him was Hunter Mason who gave him a hard punch in the face falling right into a fence. He asked for the chip peacefully before things got out of control to which Daniel refused to give. As expected for Hunter, he shows no mercy to his victims.

Although Daniel is more powerful, he was stabbed by the brass knuckle right in the stomach. It bled for a small amount of time and healed back quickly. The pain didn't last long for him. He got up, took out the brass knuckle and escaped from 3 daggers. He aimed a large amount of fire at him from the other side but Hunter Mason escaped it, and even dodged metal spikes coming out of Daniel's knuckles. Daniel looked around for Mason but by the time he was able to attack him at the last minute from behind he was tased from the front. He fell onto his knees and the recording chip was taken out of his pocket. Hunter Mason took off his hood and his mask which he threw beside him and was shocked to learn the identity of the person who went up against him. The scene crackled with tension as the towering figure loomed over Daniel. Hunter's laughter echoing ominously in the air. With a dismissive gesture after he found out he went up against a teenager in a fight. He casually destroyed the recording chip, leaving Daniel sprawled on the ground. Despite the threat and the odds stacked against him, Daniel remained defiant, his determination unyielding in the face of danger. The criminal's mocking words only fuelled his resolve, solidifying his determination to stand up against injustice, regardless of the risks. As the figure sauntered away, leaving Daniel to ponder his next move, the stage was set for a showdown between a lone teenager and the formidable forces of crime and corruption. Hunter Mason drove off, far enough to avoid being attacked anymore. Daniel was furious with himself and got up when he was able to move. He had the opportunity to destroy Hunter Mason with the current he had possessed days ago but is still unable to control it. He picked up his mask which turned back into the encrypted crystal and the pieces of the chip to see if he could rebuild it again. He picked up Clayton who was half awake and took him home. He saw Daniel without any injuries other than blood on his torn shirt. Clayton was worried as this wasn't the first time he's seen Daniel without torn clothes and blood on his body and expected an explanation but Daniel smiled at him after saving his life. In between Clayton got a massive headache and shiver inside his body while Daniel thought of another plan to find Lina Woods and the others from stealing the gem and his powers.

CHAPTER 8

As the evening wore on, Daniel had helped Clayton into his room, where he could rest after the altercation with Hunter Mason. He made up an excuse to Clayton's parents about not feeling well, citing a severe migraine. Meanwhile, Kirby Simmons, perhaps sensing that something was amiss, asked Daniel to join her in the living room, where she prepared a cup of tea for both of them. As Daniel descended the stairs, he was met with a surprising sight, someone was sitting on the couch, engaged in a conversation with Erik. To his shock, he realized that the person was Molly, his older sister. The emotional impact of seeing his long-lost sister left him beaming with joy, and Molly, too, was overwhelmed with happiness as she finally believed that her brother was alive. The two siblings embraced tightly, reuniting after months of uncertainty and fear. With Clayton resting upstairs, their parents had gone to check on him, leaving Daniel and Molly alone in the living room. Their emotions were raw, and Daniel struggled to find the right words to express his experiences during his time away. His transformation was apparent, and Molly couldn't help but notice that he had matured during their time apart. Daniel was more curious about her life over the months he was gone rather than talk about his. Molly, who was pursuing a Bachelor of Psychology at Deakin University, had also faced her share of challenges during the incident that had separated her from her brother. She had taken up online courses to support her family and care for her baby brother, Juan, all while believing that her brother was gone, despite being placed under coma. Convincing her brother to return home had been a difficult task, as Daniel needed time to adjust to his newfound circumstances and the people he had reconnected with, such as his friends from school. Despite Molly's initial disappointment at Daniel's hesitation to return immediately, she understood and respected his decision. She was told to stay and have dinner with Daniel and the rest of the family which she happily accepted before heading back home.

However, just as the night seemed to be settling down, Daniel's restlessness led him to hop out of bed and hastily put on some clothes. The bed beside him was empty, as Clayton had gone to the kitchen. Without explanation, Daniel jumped out of the window, leaving Clayton puzzled by his unexpected departure. As Clayton realized that his friend had vanished again, he noticed the open window and the pile of jumpers on the floor, signifying that something was amiss. Concerned for Daniel's well-being and confused by his behaviour, Clayton decided to follow his friend's tracks, tracking his location on his phone to find him. The night was about to take another unexpected turn, and Clayton was determined to uncover the mystery behind Daniel's actions. Daniel's sudden departure and the mysterious club visit left Clayton concerned and curious. He followed Daniel's location on his phone and found himself standing outside the club. Seeing the open window and the pile of jumpers on the floor, Clayton realized that Daniel had left in a hurry. Worried about his friend, he decided to jump out of the window and track him down. Inside the club, Daniel had already encountered two bouncers who had attempted to stop him. However, he had managed to incapacitate them, possibly indicating some hidden skills or knowledge he had acquired during his time away. As Clayton traced Daniel's location on his phone, he couldn't help but wonder about the secrets and changes that had taken place in his friend's life during the time they were apart. The reunion earlier with Molly had been a heartwarming surprise, but now there were new questions and concerns arising.

Daniel headed into the club to find the businessman who interacted with the two enemies. There were a group of men sitting at the table playing poker and betting with their money. In the next room was a club filled with people dancing and drinking at a bar across the room. The music was deafening to the ears. Another guard approached him and blocked his path, preventing him from going further. Daniel whispered his name that jogged the guard's memory and was guided into another room upstairs. In the room on the first level the place was a large room filled with artifacts and paintings of ancient roman and medieval times. Daniel spotted the view through a large window captured by the darkness of the sky and a busy street across the building. His attention went to the opened door and entered the man he was looking for who sat back in his chair. He smoked a cigar and stared blatantly at the mysterious lurker standing opposite him. His name is Salvador Harvey, a 51 year old European mafia businessman who migrated to Melbourne to run a nightclub and makes deals with people in favour of drugs, money and his name wiped off the police system. The two sat down and Daniel expected information about the Formidable Four and their whereabouts. Salvador explained to him about a deal he made with Lina Woods and Jasper Cryer about a certain weapon they are creating to secure the gem that is attached to Daniel and acquire its powers. This is what Miles wanted. Salvador knew his own capabilities, however his eye caught the attention of a bright object beaming through Daniel's jumper, which he pretended to not notice. Salvador gave him directions to the location where the weapon was made.

The eye contact and the smirk from Salavdor gave Daniel a slight suspicion that he was hiding something but the talk was done. Daniel left the building and headed to the location he was given. Clayton followed him in an uber, tracking him down while he looked confused at Daniel's actions and whereabouts. He arrived at the alleyway on 524 flinders on the other side where it was empty and quiet because the other front door was filled with shooters onsite. He phased through the building that was right in front of him and he arrived at the gambling room. The room was empty but he discovered something bigger, plans for a devastating weapon that could harness the gem's energy for mass destruction. Racing against time, he pursued leads, cracked encrypted files, and foiled attempts to assemble the dangerous weapon. Determined to protect the world from such a catastrophic threat fuelled Daniel's resolve to eliminate the remaining traces of Mile's influence. He realised that Salvador had tricked him when he heard a sound next door. Lina and Jasper were both in the room next door and the weapon was missing. Daniel was spotted by 2 shooters who entered the gambling room and he took them out. The gun shots alerted others to arrive on scene. He took out a few more shooters and looked at his surroundings for the rest. Daniel's alacrity to attack took a different approach than his original plan. He stormed in and fought Lina once again. Jasper managed to escape but not empty handed. He left with the design of the weapon but Daniel was unable to chase after him. He created lightning bolts and threw it right at Lina but it attached to her baston and rebounded right back at Daniel who was taken out. To his reactions, he knew the consequences that happened last time and the damage it created. He continued his attack on Lina even though he wanted to help her. He reached for the firearm lying on the ground next to the dead shooter. Bullets were fired at Lina who defended herself from the attack. She was unable to be found thereafter, however, attacked Daniel from behind. She repeatedly punched him and destroyed his mask in the process, however Lina nearly met her fate when she stabbed him in the chest. The gem activated and a burst of light came out of him and aimed straight at Lina who was knocked out. Daniel's mask was damaged and his face got exposed. He was yearning to kill Lina who was defenceless but was outrun by a number of shooters and Lina's assassins. She recognised him right away when she had her men surround him. She was bewildered when she saw his face, remembering how he recognised her when they first met. She also spotted the real gem attached to his chest which was revealed and created a massive hole in his jumper and to her fascination she figured out who he became. Daniel talked her out of the situation but she was too brainwashed to believe anything she heard. She ordered her men to attack but he got an opportunity to escape with a sudden realisation that he was not able to defend himself, so he escaped into the night. Daniel stood outside the club where he met Salvador Harvey. He saw him sitting on his chair on a phone call and it sounded like his plan worked, however wasn't fully pleased that the lurker was still alive. From a distance, Daniel used his blade and aimed straight through the window and right into his chest. Salvador collapsed head first on his desk and blood started streaming down.

Meanwhile, back in Undertown, Miles got hold of the weapon. He looked even more determined to kill the lurker when he found out the gem was attached right into his chest and Lina revealed his identity to him which made him more interested in his personal life in order to give up his powers by force. Daniel got a hold of Lina's mind and she agreed to meet him under Miles's command who was behind the whole ruse to gather intel. They met up in an alleyway at the back and she was extremely pleased to see him, knowing who he really is. Daniel went straight to the point and looked for answers in a much more different approach. He tried to help Lina but she was far from it and informed him that his identity was at risk but didn't explain anything further. He reached deep into her mind to let her out of the dark in search of her old memories, but the only memories he got was her un-colourful past. He demanded answers but all he got was silence from her. Daniel continued to forge any valuable information from her mind back but she denied everything and left soon after. Her stubbornness got him an opportunity to find others after he surfed through her mind. One of his clones travelled into Undertown, a town that has the black market and several types of criminals and organisations.

He spent several days getting valuable information about the situation going on and finally saw the design of the weapon. The weapon attracted any crystal magnets that would either be destroyed or used for a purpose. Meanwhile, his gem designed a new mask after the last one got damaged. It took a few days to make a new design while his clone gathered intel on the crystal magnet. 20 days without any problem, he was informed of movement outside the city, unsure of what it was about and went after the vehicle holding one potential hostage. He broke into the truck and found a familiar person strapped into the seat unable to move. It turned out to be his sister who was kidnapped, and there was a bomb attached inside the truck, in case the truck was in any way attacked by Daniel. On the bomb was a note to Daniel saying *'I know you.'* He got out of the truck and appeared right in front, destroying the four tyres. The truck didn't stop and the driver he noticed was a bald, tattooed man. The plan was a ruse to get Daniel to follow the truck and lead him to their hideout. Daniel went back inside where his sister was.

The timer hit the last 10 seconds on the bomb and was unable to be disarmed so he phased himself and Molly just in time and took her away from the explosion. It killed the driver and destroyed the truck in a failed attempt to lure Daniel to their hideout. He flew Molly back to her dorm on her request and she gave him useful information on the kidnapping where she was attacked by the driver named James Brown who kidnapped her and threw her into the back of the truck. He also injured three other students who tried to save her under Miles's command to get to Daniel but she wasn't sure what her involvement was with the Lurker. Daniel's clone continued his surveillance on the area while the real version looked out for more thugs and shooters around the university but instead the police hauled him from making his next move. He went in for questioning as he was known to be the enemy. Detective Joseph Armstrong confronted him about his recent outings and found a picture of him spotted outside the gym in Heidelberg at 11:25 pm 1 and half months ago but Daniel denied his whereabouts claiming himself to be 'studying'. They questioned his involvement with Salvador Harvey after traces of evidence led to him murdering Salvador. While this was true where the blade pierced Salvador's chest after leading him into a trap, he denied any actions he undertook as well as the recent photograph of him jumping out the window at 425 flinders lane to which he was confused about.

The detective threw him in jail and he was released until further evidence of his whereabouts was found to prove his innocence. He wasn't able to phase through walls or bars as that would expose his identity he's been trying to hide for 3 months. A couple of days later the police were given photographic evidence regarding the movement of the mist around the streets and intended to go after it but weren't able to chase after him as it disappeared after the police went after him in 8 blocks, it later turned out to be his clone commanded through a conversation held in Daniel's mind who went out of his way from his current mission to help Daniel from being incriminated by the judge. Over in Undertown, Lina and Jasper walked in the night together searching for a potential spy lurking around, sourcing for information. This information was given to Miles who realised that the shadow that followed him a few days prior was a spy who was fishing for information about them and it helped him track down what he believed to be a lurker. Smoke bombs were thrown at Lina and Jasper by what appeared to be an un-masked vigilante who could be seen running off. Lina and Jas-per separated on either side to find the vigilante and was finally captured by Jasper from one end near the warehouse and Lina found the two of them. However, Lina failed to aim at the clone's throat and her knife flew behind Jasper. The clone es-caped and while Jasper blamed himself, he turned around to find Lina but caught her by surprise when she stabbed him and ruptured his lower intestines. She gently left him bleeding on the floor and ran away to avoid her cover from being blown up.

A few days later, there was no evidence that proved that Daniel was the lurker and he was given bail from Clayton's par-ents. At that time, Daniel was unable to get any information from his clone. The chip's camera died and he was not able to reach out. The following afternoon, Principal Bell's conversa-tion with other teachers of a hooded and masked individual running around the school had reached Daniel's ears because of his supersonic hearing, and he feared that she might have him in her sights. Believing she had been watching him closely due to his irregular attendance at school, he contemplated leaving the school altogether. However, Clayton's interruption put a stop to his escape plan, and the worried expression in Clayton's eyes suggested he had some concerning information to share.. Clayton showed Daniel a recent photograph of him outside the club, and a cold shiver ran down Daniel's spine as he realized his secret life as a vigilante might be exposed. Dan-iel reluctantly shared his story with Clayton who initially dis-played mixed emotions as he realised that it was his tracking that led the investigators to Daniel's whereabouts, and assume he is the lurker, hence his brief arrest. Although Daniel was irri-tated with Clayton for his actions, he had a change of heart and asked for his help. Clayton agreed, and the two embarked on a tram ride, with Clayton catching up on the recent events Daniel had uncovered. The chip remained non-functional, and Daniel was unable to communicate with his clone, leaving him anxious about the clone's fate. As the tram headed to the city, a group of masked men appeared on the roof, and a black car followed closely behind. Daniel's heightened senses allowed him to detect the danger, and he spotted a passenger in the car pulling out a gun. With quick thinking, he subtly controlled the tram door, incapacitating both the driver and the shooter. However, moments later, another attack occurred, and the tram came under heavy fire. Bullets flew, and the tram was surrounded by shooters from all sides. Daniel and Clayton, along with several other passengers, took cover as chaos erupted. Eight individuals managed to escape the scene, including Clayton, while three unfortunate souls lost their lives. Daniel, however, was not swift enough to fend off the attackers this time, and he was knocked out cold before being taken away. Inside the tram, Clayton discovered the tracking chip, now stained with blood. He decided to keep it with him, intending to repair it and use it to locate Daniel, who had been captured and taken away, leaving his fate uncertain. The story took an even darker and more perilous turn, with Clayton left as Daniel's only hope for rescue.

Daniel found himself unable to escape in the dull deepness of Undertown. In front of him was a group of black market buyers and hackers looking to separate the gem from his chest by attaching a magnet on it. His wrists had steel cuffs that prevented him from using his invisibility powers to escape. Straight ahead of him was his clone, dead as a crooked door nail. His neck snapped and his body lay on the chair. The camera on his chest was destroyed into pieces. It made more sense why the chip failed and he didn't receive any information in the last 4 days. Miles was upset with the clone spy crawling around his territory, but he raged when he saw the one behind the mask. The weapon was ready after numerous tests and Daniel had no other way out. Meanwhile Lina the second mole tailing Mile's operation who killed her former partner which saved Daniel's clone was making her own moves. The conversation between her and Daniel struck her mind and she had a change of heart. She had been gathering information and monitoring the situation from the shadows. Realizing the immense threat Miles posed not only to Daniel but to the entire city and possibly the world, she decided to take matters into her own hands. Her loyalties were no longer with Miles, and she sought to help Daniel escape his clutches.

Fro Jha's voice continued to echo in his mind, Daniel realized that this was his only chance to escape the dire situation he found himself in. As the magnet was brought closer to him, Daniel used his newfound miniature form to his advantage. He deftly slipped through the gaps between the steel cutlers on his wrists, now small enough to manoeuvre effortlessly. Miles powered the weapon and aimed right at his chest. Sensing an opportunity, summoning every ounce of concentration, Daniel focused on the power within him, the ability to manipulate his size at will, a power he can use when required. Remembering the words spoken by Fro Jha and within seconds to spare when Miles pulled the trigger, he willed himself to shrink, and to his amazement, he felt his body respond. Gradually, he became smaller and smaller until he was no bigger than a pebble, hid den from the view of the weapon aimed at him.

The blast created a hole in the wall and a few seconds of smile on Miles's face changed when the dust cleared. All he saw was an empty chair, no gem and three of his men dead on the ground with a blade stuck to their chest and blood dripping quickly.. As he watched over the bodies, he discovered a familiar weapon and sent Hunter Mason to find Lina. Meanwhile Daniel changed back into normal size and deployed a counter attack on Miles. He looked extremely confused at every attack and punch that came at him and right in front of him was Daniel who sped off while Miles followed him. Tensions filled the air due to Lina's ability to blend into shadows and strike from unexpected angles. Following her is Hunter Mason, who favours a more direct approach, using his brute force. The body of Jasper Cryer hung by the neck on the rope above did not frighten Mason but made him more determined to kill Lina without hesitation after her betrayal towards the Formidable Four. Lina looked to battle her way out of the fight and break out into the night. She found a vehicle but saw a bomb in the front seat and it exploded instantly. Lina survived despite burns on her arms and she was approached by Hunter Mason who looked disappointed but didn't care enough to see her alive. The confrontation began in a dimly lit abandoned warehouse, with beams of moonlight piercing through the broken windows. Lina moved silently, her footsteps nearly imperceptible as she scanned her surroundings. Hunter Mason, armed with an assortment of daggers and a wicked grin, confidently stepped forward, taunting Lina with his superiority. Lina relies on her expertise in hand-to-hand combat and her quick reflexes, aiming to outmanoeuvre her opponent. She struck with calculated precision, landing blows and retreating before Hunter could respond. Her agility and evasive manoeuvres kept her one step ahead, making it difficult for Hunter to get a clean shot at her. Lina manages to disarm Hunter of one of his daggers and destroys his brass knuckles. Gaining a momentary advantage, she slits his throat. Unable to move or catch his breath the invincible, inevitable one of most fearsome international murderer was killed at the hands of Lina, breaking the Formidable Four one by one. Meanwhile, Miles did not give up he fought till his last bullet, trying to provoke the moving shadow on the wall but unable to find Daniel in the process. He was approached by Lina who distracted him through the alleyway, a plan made by Daniel himself. The two fought in a one on one battle and as Miles stood the higher ground, he was shot in the arm by a machine gun attached to the side of the rear on the vehicle and his weapon was taken away, giving them enough time to escape from Undertown before Miles hunted them down again. Clayton drove through the tunnels and into the night, finding a location that would take them off the grid.

CHAPTER 9

Miles's situation had taken a turn for the worse. He was now on his own, betrayed and wounded, with a fierce adversary in the form of Lina Woods, who was now against him. Miles' determination to secure the gem remained unwavering, and he had secured a strand of black hair in his possession, which he hoped would provide him with some crucial information. As he waited for the results from the lab, Miles took care of his injuries. His arm was strapped tightly, the pain from the injuries served as a constant reminder of the treacherous situation he was in when he was purposely hit by a car as a distraction to escape. Two long nights passed, with Miles growing increasingly anxious as he awaited the results. The lack of answers was testing his patience, and He was frustrated and waited for the results impatiently when finally at 3.00am the computer beeped and he got the results, he could not be more happier. Relief washed over him, knowing that he was one step closer to achieving his goal. The following day, Miles realized that he had no one to rely on for support but found some of the guys Hunter Mason worked with as backup to locate Lina Woods. Oddly, he heard no response from them and Miles was left with no choice but to face the challenges ahead on his own, fully aware that the odds were stacked against him. His determination and the information he had acquired from the black hair were his only allies in the dangerous game he was playing. As the city's skyline shimmered under the twilight sky, Clayton and Daniel drove to the Yarra river, carrying the crystal magnet they had taken with them for it to be destroyed. Daniel set the timer of the bomb to

20 seconds and tipped the weapon in. A large splash of water gushed from the bottom and merely 20 seconds later a high tide of waves crashed on shore, causing a small flood on the pathway before it became puddle and part of the walk bridge temporarily collapsed due to the after effects of the explosion with no casualties, however it got the attention of many people and angry workers, but no one really knew who or what caused the problem. Police and reporters arrived soon after but Daniel and Clayton disappeared. Daniel and Clayton went their separate ways and he sent Clayton home for observation on his computer checking the location of Lina Woods and any mishaps on the latest stint from Miles. Daniel couldn't get inside her mind but got a text message from Clayton on her whereabouts. He got on the earliest train to Mornington where she was. There he found the rehabilitation centre and went inside.

The place was spacious in spite of broken windows, rough floors and large blue rusty walls which meant the place was abandoned. In front of him was a projector and a screen in black and white. He realised there was a video and the first thing he saw was a house, a house near a very familiar waterfront. In the backyard is an infant playing with a dad and inside a mother cooking in the kitchen. The screen was now zoomed in and in the kitchen was a familiar person Daniel was slightly able to recognise, and after some thinking he realised Miles's final plan. He found a person sitting on the chair and he immediately decided to go for the attack. Sitting on the chair was a dummy and a message - *The final act...* Daniel, battered and wounded, found himself in a dire situation. The revelation that his own family believed he was dead had ignited a fire within him, pushing him to confront the perilous circumstances surrounding him. As he moved through the shadows, the lack of control over the darkness revealed a vulnerability he hadn't fully mastered. Driven by a mix of determination and desperation, Daniel ambushed the first person he encountered after leaving the room where he read the damning message. However, the darkness betrayed him, and he fell into a trap, a blade unexpectedly piercing his ribs. The agony intensified as he endured the relentless cycle of healing and subsequent stabbings, each assault chipping away at his resolve. The torturers sought information about Lina Woods' whereabouts and perhaps an exchange for the worst thing that could happen next. Daniel, in his weakened state, was forced to endure the torment. The cruel twist of fate exposed Miles's ominous plan, an impending threat to Daniel's family. The images on the screen served as a painful reminder of his powerlessness and his absence. In his lowest moment as he was on the brink of giving up, lying in a pool of his own blood, Daniel heard a familiar, comforting voice. Fro Jha's voice and then spirited body emerged from the shadows, advising him to press on, to find strength in the midst of despair.

As Daniel shook his head and saw hope towards him, the ethereal guidance urged him to rise, to face the challenges ahead with patience, the foundational skill in both power and combat. As Fro Jha's presence dissipated, his voice lingered, echoing words of encouragement that stirred a newfound hope within Daniel. Despite the physical and emotional toll, Daniel, still on his knees, embraced the guidance and struggled to find the strength to carry on. The battle was far from over, but within the echoes of Fro Jha's advice, Daniel discovered the resilience to endure and the will to continue his fight. When two of Miles's men returned they found only a pool of blood and moments later, a blade caught through a collar of the shirt of one guy and the other found his bones snapped by baston. Both were clueless about their opponent, but soon Daniel gained his power to get to his invisible form and he left the premises without being sighted. Night began to fall when Daniel raced back home. It was a cold evening just closer to midnight. Daniel cleaned the stains of blood from his jumper. He was a couple of meters away from the vacant Bentley parked at the back of the house and saw movement near the garage. One of Mile's men, formerly commanded by Hunter Mason, had his sister and she was forced to open the garage door. The two went in and Daniel was able to see through as she was leaning towards the wall with the gun pointed directly on her head. The other man guarded the front door and there was no sign or movement from Miles or his parents. He noticed the man guarding the front door. Daniel jumped off the roof of the house next door and sprayed a large amount of mist out of his palm. It grabbed the attention of the guard and he saw a brief reflection in motion through the gas and started firing bullets. In seconds he passed out from the mist and his pulse was beating slower than normal. The toxic mist continued to spread throughout the neighbourhood, although people were unaware of it as the mist prevented them from seeing Daniel or the house being under attack created by the shield replicated by the gem. Inside the house there was no sign of movement detected in the front room, however a noise echoed through from upstairs. The sound of footsteps got louder coming down as Daniel went up and a few moments later felt a gunshot in his chest. He fell down from top to bottom and while his chest healed quickly from the wound, his left knee shattered into pieces as he collapsed. Daniel lay on the ground, his chest still throbbing from the gunshot wound that had already begun to heal. His shattered knee sent waves of pain through his body, rendering him unable to move as Miles's menacing presence loomed over him which made him realise that even though immortality prevents him from a certain near death, he is still part human. Blood trickled from his lips, Jasper was unable to move as he suffered enduring pain from the broken knee. Miles's eyes gleamed with triumph as he looked down, relishing in the suffering he had inflicted. With a swift motion, he reached towards Daniel's chest, his fingers closing around the gem embedded there and threw him onto the wall. But instead of seizing the gem and claiming its power for himself he so desires, Miles paused. He knew that there were more painful ways to break Daniel, more cruel methods to crush his spirit. With a gesture, Miles called the men from the garage, emerging like shadows from the darkness. Among them were Daniel's family, held captive and trembling with fear, guns pointed to their heads. Daniel's heart clenched at the sight of them, his sister's eyes wide with terror, his parents' faces pale with shock. He longed to protect them, to shield them from the horrors. but his shattered body betrayed him. Miles mentioned he secretly created a powerful cap and created copies that prevented the individual from being seen or attacked. They can go through walls and other solid structures without a time limit. A similar design created by the gem which allows Daniel to do the same but without the use of a cap. The caps were put on by both men except the one who was in the garage. It was planned and the two men had seen Daniel coming in from the roof.

They were both in the truck which was parked behind the neighbouring house. The sight of his family, held captive and frightened, only fuelled his desperation. Miles's offer hung heavy in the air, a cruel ultimatum dangling before Daniel which was to reveal himself to his family, to relinquish the gem and allow Miles to seize control of it by controlling the city which he travelled so far from and the world he expects to be his or to watch helplessly as his whole family unaware of their son and sibling amongst them, lying injured, gasping for breath suffered the consequences of his defiance. In the midst of the chaos and fear, Daniel's mind raced. His thoughts flickered between the safety of his family and the weight of the responsibility thrust upon him that he swore to protect. Could he bear to betray everything he stood for, to surrender the gem and grant Miles the power he so ruthlessly sought? Or would he find the strength to resist, to endure whatever suffering lay ahead, knowing that his family's lives hung in the balance? With each passing moment, the pressure mounted. Daniel's heart pounded in his chest, torn between conflicting desires, torn between love and duty, between sacrifice and survival. But in the end, as he looked into the eyes of his family, their fear mirrored his own, Daniel knew that there was no choice at all. With a steely resolve, he braced himself against the pain, against the fear, and made his decision. He painfully and slowly got up, leaning his back on the wall.

CHAPTER 10

H is face started to sweat and went through with the pain. He took off his hood and his mask which was the exact thing Miles asked him to do. When his face was exposed, his family was stunned. His sister smiled at him when she realised it was her brother who saved her from the kidnapping that day and his parents were relieved to see him alive. Miles's smile exceeded fear, but Daniel didn't look pleased. With a swift and decisive motion, Daniel drew out his baston, its blades appearing on both ends. Ignoring the pain that shot through his battered knee, he hopped to his right, his mind focused solely on the safety of his family. Daniel lunged towards the two men who held his parents captive, his baston spinning in a deadly dance of steel. With each strike, he carved through their defences, his movements fuelled by a fierce determination. The men, caught off guard by Daniel's sudden burst of strength, faltered under his relentless assault. With a series of precise strikes, Daniel disarmed them, sending their weapons clattering to the ground before delivering a final blow that sent them sprawling to the floor. But wasting no time, Miles lost an immense amount of patience. He drew out his gun and immediately shot Daniel's parents. Daniel's heart clenched with horror as he watched helplessly, his body still weakened from his earlier ordeal. His sister looked on as tears rolled down her eyes and she started screaming in pain. Daniel went up to his parents who were gasping for air. Blood spread through the floor. Daniel's dad died instantly, but his mum had life left in her. Miles reloaded his gun once again, as he pointed it towards his sister. Daniel turned around to see his sister one last time not sure if he can save her. He couldn't move as quickly as he wanted. Suddenly a voice echoed through him, the same voice from the rehab centre. He had remembered Fro Jha's words to find the strength inside him. Daniel took a few deep breaths, he remembered the memories from his younger days, the strength he found in him with his family and friends and soon he remembered a task he had to complete while inside the gem. Miles still gave Daniel the opportunity to give him the gem and avoid bloodshed. Once again, Daniel turned down his request and this pissed Miles's off even more, with a vein that appeared on his forehead. He got angrier and clicked the gun. Molly closed her eyes. The bullet was fired but it didn't hit her. Molly opened her eyes once again, life flashed before her thinking her time was over, but she saw no wound or blood on her body. Instead, the bullet floated in thin air, hardly able to move.

Daniel stuck his palm out controlling the bullet. His mind was focused solely on that and nothing more, and soon vaporized the bullet into thin air, the only thing left was the gunpowder that fell on the floor. Molly was amazed, she was saved from death by her brother. Daniel took down Miles and strapped him and the rest of his men outside his van and called the police and the ambulance. The mist disappeared and the house was seen by many people as a crime scene. Daniel went up to his parents, his mum still alive from the gunshot. She smiled at him and was happy to see him after the months that separated them apart. The ambulance arrived, but Daniel's mum turned to him one last time. She started crying, unable to gasp for more breath. She whispered to him the secret to her still being alive. While in her human form, she had the ability to heal people from a sudden death or injury. A power so unusual it was forged in the shadows of the gem itself. She told Daniel of an accident that happened 10 years ago, but she wasn't given all the powers in that gem, but she discovered the ability to heal people during her job one day in the hospital that was beyond her understanding. A power that forced her to see a psychologist who helped her get over the voices in her mind who were no longer alive and a healer. The healer she saw was an ancient man. a man with a white beard who claimed to be a peacekeeper of death and destruction. Daniel knew that man, as Fro Jha, who his mum had encountered years ago. The power she had was limited and she didn't have immortality like Daniel and the power came with a price. She was told that if she was ever shot or stabbed, the power inside her wouldn't heal her and once that was released, she wouldn't survive. That's when Daniel's realised that encounter with the gem was no accident. It clearly meant Fro Jha was looking for another person which was in his prophecy. In her final moments, she released her power by memorising a few ancient words. She touched the gem on his chest and a breeze of light came out of her body and was captured by the gem. A new power given to him to heal the injured and those who would have suffered a near death experience. She smiled at him, proud of how far he came with his new abilities. She touched his smooth face and wiped the tears of him. Then died in his arms as her pulse stopped. A reunion that didn't last forever, was cherished. Both were taken to the hospital to be examined and looked at before preparing for the funeral. Daniel reunited once again with his sister who hugged him for saving her from death. She was ecstatic to have a brother who would help people and look after the city. He met his brother for the first time who was asleep in his crib and he carried him in his arms despite blood on his hands. Daniel was also taken to hospital later on to deal with his knee injury that ruled him out of the whole summer as he wasn't able to play cricket. The house was now in ruins and the three siblings needed a new place to live. Molly had a place near her university and lived with her brothers in that house. It was a spacious apartment near the city, with 3 bedrooms and a brilliant view. Originally it was shared with Molly and her friends but after the whole situation that occurred a few days prior the decision had been changed. The incident was reported as a midnight robbery that killed Daniel's parents which was far from the truth. Daniel avoided any more conflict and denied all rumours that went on about him. 3 weeks before Christmas, the funeral was held at the general cemetery outside the city. Families came down from Sydney, London and some of them from the Netherlands. Daniel wore a moonboot, following the dreaded news that he was unable to do any physical activities for most of the summer, being told that his knee would take a couple of months to heal. He met up with his best friend, Clayton and his girlfriend Anya who came to the funeral to offer their condolences. Daniel gave a moving speech about his parents' lives as people mourned the loss of Daniel's parents Michael Steele and Dr Liz McPhee, a successful accountant and a doctor at the Royal children's hospital, who were respected and loved for their personality and successful careers. He paid a glowing tribute to his mother who was a warm loving mother however he couldn't tell everyone the real truth about her, which only his friend Clayton and sister Molly knew. The audience gracefully clapped and the coffin was buried into the ground.

A few weeks into the new year, Daniel used his gem to create him a new suit that allowed him to turn on and turn off when he liked. An electric powered helmet that doesn't break in a battle and armoured metal robes. His gem also created new headquarters in his apartment that he used, to follow Fro Jha's mission to protect the world from death, darkness, destruction. In the meantime his mind had led to something else and it was bothering him for a few days. He visited the prison that Miles was in. Holding no grudge against him, Daniel calmly listened to what he had to say. Miles told him of what's coming. An early prophecy he was told when he met someone bigger than him through the shadows in the mountains of East Asia who has professed a child would bear certain powers and be claimed as the child of the underworld demon that will bring a darker future. When asked if he saw the face of this person, he denied, other than he described his voice as deep and he roared through the shadows. A beast that was flooding Daniel's mind earlier while he was in the gem which saw death, destruction and darkness. This caused the fear inside of him. He may have seen the future, a darker future of what lies ahead.

ABOUT THE AUTHOR

When I was in junior school, I put in some thought and creativity in authoring a short story about two kids involved in time travel, which got published a year later and now is placed in some libraries in Mumbai and Melbourne. Before that I never knew I had talent in writing. Some of my best accomplishments are mainly in the sporting world, which involved some prestigious awards in cricket and basketball and an academic award in school. I always believed that this academic award was due to my greatest achievements in English and literature as well as other subjects.